I0619302

Elias Presents:
LITTLE BLACK BOOK

ISBN 978-0-578-64495-0

Elias Presents:
LITTLE BLACK BOOK

By
Poetic Art

Elias Shabazz
2020

Copyright © 2020 by Elias Shabazz

All rights reserved. This book or any portion thereof may not be reproduced or used in any manner whatsoever without the express written permission of the publisher except for the use of brief quotations in a book review or scholarly journal.

First Printing: 2020

ISBN 978-0-578-64495-0

Elias Shabazz
mr.eliasshabazz@gmail.com

Dedication

To the best version of myself.
I Thank you.
With patience, vision, and encouragement.
I have achieved my dream.

Contents

Foreword

After reading this masterpiece of literary artistry. It is a great honor to express my admiration for the work compiled in this book. The soul and essence of the author has brought life to poetry in a way to appeal on connections of the opposite sex. You will enjoy too clever usage of phrases and expressions that test your levels of vibration from head to toe. He has served the public with words that will help you say things that commands love and affection. This is a great book of poetry made conducive on a cruise, candlelight dinner or any event, private or public to seal your union. Enjoy and dare to be romantically bold to heart of your mate or significant other.

Cleveland Palmer
Art Professor

Preface

I can remember how the beginning was. My memory is vivid. My mother would tell me that I was born with an "old soul". Looking in the rearview mirror, I can see what she meant. It took me some time for my chronological age to catch up to the age of my old soul. I venture to say that it also took just as long of a time for my psychological age, romantic, and poetic heart to catch up to my chronological age as well. At the age of nine I was beginning to write secret admirer letters to the girls that I liked in school. I did that from grade school until a few months after high school. Looking back, I know that I was writing to girls in a way that they had not yet understood how to receive. I was different. That was ok though. I simply kept writing and imagining. By age ten I was entering the seventh grade. I was being romantically crafted and inspired to write what I was feeling from new faces and interactions. I was quiet. I was non assuming. It was a new experience. I had little friends. I was overweight, younger, and shorter than everyone. I was overlooked by nearly all. Fortunately for me I had natural gifts that would galvanize my classmates and me.

When I was a little boy, I discovered that I was able to express myself through art. My brothers and I would spend many hours drawing our favorite comic book superheroes, cartoon characters, and creating some of our own. Through the years our artwork improved by leaps and bounds. My older brother cultivated his art from graphite artwork to paintings. I loved looking at how he would start his process from a sketch, to a full-on life like painting of his favorite sports athlete. It was during this time that my art shifted to another genre. I was twelve years old.

My mother gave me a book to read. It was called, "The Creative Writer". Inside this book is where I gravitated to writing as an art form and begin taking writing just as serious as I took drawing. I was particularly enamored with poetry. There were writings and passages from well-known writers of poetry, plays, and literature such as Elizabeth Barrett-Browning, Robert Browning, Miguel de Cervantes, Edmond Rostand, TS Elliot, Edgar Allen Poe, and all of

William Shakespeare's tragedies and sonnets. This book opened my mind to different perspectives. I approached writing differently. I started to write from the vantage point of the reader. I wanted my words to flow melodically while reaching the core of the reader. I wanted to mesmerize. To captivate. To grasp the mind of my audience. My thesaurus became my best writing friend. I would still write secret admirer letters. Only now I would write them to older girls. I would leave letters on my friends' older sisters' car and their friends' car. The reactions that I received encouraged me to keep writing and cultivating my skills. They loved them. Especially considering no one talked to them in the type language that a wrote. To this day. They still do not know it was me. I would often play the role of Cyrano. Providing words for my friends to give to their girlfriends. However; I was still seeking the approval of the young ladies at my high school. They were the immediate approximate to having a connection with the fairer sex. Unfortunately for me. I graduated high school the same way I entered. Without consideration.

Welcome to the Harlem Renaissance. I am now out of high school and my mind is like a sponge for art appreciation. I began reading everything that I could get my hands on. Hemingway, Hawthorne, and F. Scott Fitzgerald. I had been inundated to these literary influences early on in life through the machinations of the American school system. My real learning and education had always remained inside my home. My mind was free to immerse myself in what I liked and desired. No more studying and reading for the sake of a grade. I gave my full attention to Langston Hughes, Nikki Giovanni, Zora Neale Hurston, Maya Angelou, Pablo Neruda, Jacob Lawrence, Nina Simone, and so many more. As it relates to literature, art, poetry, and music. If the Creative Writer allowed me to write from the readers perspective. Then the artist from the Harlem Renaissance and those who followed thereafter, allowed me to write from the heart broken. The downtrodden. The invisible people who speaks not. When I was younger. Guys would put girls phone numbers in their "little black book". I put poetry in mine.

I have been writing LITTLE BLACK BOOK for what seem to be a lifetime. It is a culmination of beauty, despair, unrequited love, happiness, and freedom. This book has been trapped in my mind waiting for time to set it free. There have been several iterations that were scrapped, salvaged, and then scrapped again. All this was for the sake of giving it life.   LITTLE BLACK BOOK is the embodiment of my childhood crushes, love letters, and disappointments having evolved to maturity.   The level of understanding that I have been fortunate to achieve, and process is priceless. LITTLE BLACK BOOK is meant to welcome everyone to a good time. It is meant to be enjoyed with smiles, intrigue, openness, gasps, and sexual tension. To some, it is meant to say. Look at me now.

I am now taller. I maintain my health. More than anything. I am not quiet anymore. My voice is strong, unapologetic, confident, and I have something to say. In LITTLE BLACK BOOK, my words are precise, deliberate, and well thought out. I do not waste my words. So, give me your undivided attention. I am a man that no longer admires in secrecy. If I am writing to or about you. I mean for you to know who I am. I have taken my journey to and through college, speaking events, and spoken word platforms. I am humble and at ease. Eager to share what has been created from my mind. Allow me to introduce myself.

Poetic Art

Introduction

I am writing this book to let the world know what happens when a mannish little boy becomes a well-versed and cultured man. I write like I speak and talk how I write. Literature is very sexy. Poetry is my art. Spoken word is my language. To all who reads this. It is only the start.

Poetry, spoken word, and literature. These artistic expressions of the creative mind are more than simple words. The heart, soul and the mind are combined to produce the freedom of self. Profound play on words are the byproduct of innermost and guarded secrets. Secrets of love, pain, passion, laughter, erotica, happiness, and sex.

These readings are intended for the mature mind. Quite simply, this is for "grown folks". However, I would like all adults to find their place within my words. I want ladies to enjoy all the facets that this book has to offer. Read it alone with your favorite bottle of wine or join in with others for discussions. Gentlemen be inspired to use this book as your voice during times when you may be lost for words. Welcome to the world of my Little Black Book.

P A
Los Angeles, CA
December, 2019

ORIGINAL FANTASY (PART ONE)

You are the Original Fantasy

Let it be known and be spoken strong.

When my lips contact your body.

Everything be right and not wrong.

It is mid-day and my mind cannot stay away from thoughts of you.

Erotic interpretations of love making

Got me lying in bed shaking.

You are the Original Fantasy

That is thirty years in the making.

I thought I was forsaken,

But then I saw

That you were ready to be taken.

Grabbed and caressed by these hands of mine.

All I needed was just a little time.

THE LETTER

Dear Ginger,

I collect and gather my spiritual center with the means and aims for you to enter. My intimate place. Your intimate space. We are like governing electrons orbiting one another. Your gravity is pulling me uninterrupted with a magnetic attraction that is pushing me towards the embrace of a lifetime. I allow nature to connect us like beads on a string. I admire the mathematical equation of your design. Dynamic curves, equilateral angles and symmetry. Royalty that needs to be within my circumference permanently. You are not an elliptical illusion. You are real as numbers and as tangible as my pulsating frame. Shall I repeat it again. Ginger is your name. I speak your name allowed and sweet flavors set upon my tongue. I can taste you. I visualize you and I feel the warmth of the sun. I can see you. I inhale the breath of your sensuality and you are oxygenating every cell of my body. I am alive with you. The rhythm of our bodies is entangled with the pleasures and joys of one another. I can touch you. I am captivated by every word that you whisper to my soul. I can hear you. Are you ready? Can you take it? If not. Please don't fake it. Because all men are not created equal. Once is not enough for me. I require exponential sequels. Part 1 through parts 10. The words you speak is "daddy" do it again. Parts 10 through parts 20. The words you speak is "daddy" it's plenty. Laying on your stomach I soak into you deeply. Laying on your back I speak to and massage your center repeatedly. Fulfilling your pleasure receptors completely. Vivid is my world and my imagination have no measure. When it is all said and done. It is Ginger that I treasure.

Life is Love,
Poetic Art

SECOND LETTER

Dear Simone,

I feel free and liberated when I write. Time suspends itself momentarily. Within these moments in time I can pull ideas and meaningful content from my higher self. Articulating my wants and desires. My aches and my pains. My smiles and laughter. I am in my truest state of honesty. I write what I am feeling. I am unapologetic by this. Life can be fleeting and like a vapor. Dissipating and vanishing before my eyes. For this I tend to seize opportunities when it presents itself. I am one who believe in one in a million or even a billion opportunity. The fact that I can speak to you and you to me is a manifestation of such. Out of millions. We seized the opportunity of life and are now basking in the sunlight. I have lots of writings that I want to share with you. I am a man that's mean everything I say. And I tend to say what I mean. In another time before so much technology. I would be writing a letter to you with romance, love, and candor. And I would be on pins and needles yearning in anticipation for your reply in the mail.

Peace and Love,
Poetic Art

WHEN ITS ON ITS ON

When it's on it's on.
I feel the strength of my ancient ancestors feeling me up.
My blood is in a rush and pumping hard.
My ebony flesh is drawn to your caress.
You are so beautiful, sweet, and black.
Slow down so I can massage your back.
I know you want it, need it, and got to have it.
If you are not careful, I will become your habit.
Do you like what you see?
Do you like what I got?
I know you like how I keep it wet and hot.
Hot like lava, and wet like rain.
The tears in my eyes are from pleasure not pain.
You make me shake and shiver,
With every touch you deliver.
Bless me with a kiss from your luscious lips,
And sanctify me with the smooth rotation of your hips.
You taste so good from the bottom to top.
If I hold my eruption any longer, I'll damn sure pop.
Hold me and don't move.
Don't move and I'll hold you.
With the love we make, we are one from two.
Our bond is eternal.
Your passion is an inferno.
You are a prize to my eyes,
Leaving me Hypnotized.
There is always tomorrow and more where this come from.
When it's on it's on,
You leave me blind, deaf, and dumb.

CHOCOLATE DIPPED, CARAMEL THICK, AND HONEY SWEET

Dear Shannine,

I have an infatuation and need of your sweet taste. The enticement of my fantasies begins with the delicious joy you bring. You have a bursting asunder of sexual flavors. I have a bursting sensation from your intimate favors. My chocolate stiffness inside your caramel thickness, ripples the nerves of my satisfaction down my spine. I have a sweet tooth for the honey taste between your legs. I have deep roots for the way you make me beg. Your Chocolate, Caramel and Honey complexions. Swells my manhood to the point of vibrating erections. My Chocolate melts in your mouth. While your Caramel sticks to my tongue. My eyes are glazed over from your Honey love. You are one of a kind, and your love is second to none.

One Love,
Poetic Art

THE LIGHT OF DAY

As the light of day awaken me to a new sunrise.
I feel the joy of your presence when I open my eyes.
Lying next to you, listening to the bird's song of spring.
I often pinch myself to make sure you are the real thing.
A heavenly delight is what you appear to me.
I know I'm not perfect,
But you are perfect for me.
From the very first time I blessed my eyes on you.
I knew that you were my only temptation.
My midnight craving.
My morning appetite.
You are the ease to my pain that make everything right.
Precious are the moments when we are alone.
From holding your hand,
 To the smile of your face.
I feel alive within your warm embrace.
As the light of day is replaced by a moonlit night.
I feel the joy of your presence
When holding you tight.

KEEP IT REAL

Forever in love with you.......The hell with this. Scratch that!!!! Let
me keep this real.

Let us get this straight and keep it real.
You know I keep your pussy wet with satisfaction.
You know the deal.

I'm big daddy long stroke.
I'm thick dick black.
I know you are addicted to me
Like an addict is addicted to crack.
When I'm inside you I can feel your wetness,
Flowing with orgasmic contractions.
I'm a verb.
I do my thang with action.

I am no joke. Now let me keep it real.
You are the truth girl.
Hell nah. You are the shit!
You know I keep your pussy wet when I massage your clit.
It's not your choice to get moist.
You couldn't help it if you wanted to.

I'm thick dick black.
I'm big daddy long stroke.
If you need to be blazed, heated, or have your fire lit.
Just keep it real baby girl.
I'm the Muthafuckin Shit!!

WOMAN IS MY BALANCE

The balance between us is non yielding,
Nor does it tilt.
We are fashioned and forged,
From innocence and guilt.
The balance from Ying to Yang, or rain to sunshine.
I know if I'd scratch your back.
You would scratch mine.
You are my woman and I love you deep.
I ache to be in your arms,
And crave you in my sleep.
I cherish you to the way that I breathe life.
Without the utterance of words, spoken or written.
I am afflicted with love by all that is you.
You are my woman and you balance me strong.
I am a shell of myself,
Without you to right me when I'm wrong.
You are the heat of my night.
As I am the cool in your day.
Yang and Ying.
You are my Queen.
Balancing her King.
You are my woman and you balance me right.
I am connected to you
Even when we disagree and fight.
In your smile I lose my frown.
You raise me up when my emotions are down.
Your love is priceless.
I can never fight this.
The truth of my woman is the balance of a lie.
I am free to be me. To laugh or cry.
To walk or run.
Play in the sun.
You balance today, tonight, yesterday and tomorrow.
With all my love for you.
Your shine ignites my happiness,
And remove my pains and sorrow.

SWEET TOOTH

Dear Jacque,

Face down. Ass up. Chocolate KISSES never misses. I know how you like to be sucked and fucked. I will eat you NOW and LATER. Because you are GOOD and PLENTY. Your KIT KAT purrs and talks with me. So, it is a must that I speak in tongues. ABBA-ZABA ABBA-ZABA. Fuck it! Where do I start? You cum in my mouth and taste like SWEET TARTS. Fuck it! Where do I begin? You nut on my chin in a MILKY WAY repeatedly. Again, and again. My dick is hard, and my veins are thick like RED VINES throbbing and pulsating. Don't keep me waiting. Suck me like a BLOW POP. When life gives us lemons. You give me Original LEMONHEAD. But I have a better idea instead. When I ejaculate. Take a shot of my DNA and drink a BIT-O-HONEY. You are my ALMOND JOY. I am your HERSHEY DARK CHOCOLATE. My erection is perfection. Because when I see your pussy. I keep popping it.

Forget Me Not,
Poetic Art

ANATOMY OF A MID-SUMMER NIGHT

It seems as if the thermometer has broken and popped. That's how hot it is tonight. The temperature must be just below the century mark. It is past midnight and the heat is exhausting. I lay in bed turning and tossing. There is a rapping and a tapping and a knock at my door. My naked body is mist with perspiration as I walk across the floor. Who could this be at this hour of the night? I open the door to a pleasant delight of sight. She is standing in my doorway. Her body is tight, firm, and ripe. She said it was too hot and could not relax   to   sleep. She thought the same of me and felt the desire to see. She wears next to nothing as she crosses the other side of my threshold. I notice and see what her intentions are for me. My body and thoughts are electrified. She is carrying a small bucket of ice cubes and ice chips. She said that she came to cool me off. But instead I begin to feel a fire inside. A burning eruption of a roaring flame. The temperature became a fleeting thought in my mind. All I could think of was the many ways we would achieve multiple orgasms. Verbal communications were not needed on this night. Nonverbal exchanges are the language of choice. Followed by physical reassurance, a strong back and high endurance. She fluttered my body with erotic kisses. From the top of my crown to my feet, and everywhere in between. She did not miss. I reciprocated likewise. She dropped to her knees and placed me in her mouth. She sucked my soul. I laid her on her back and licked her emotions. It was real Funkadelic. I played the six and she played the nine. Our bodies were in a passionate bliss suspended in time. The length of my touch was received by the center of her depth. She pulled out of me the nectar of my heritage. The juice of my legacy. I studied her body like it was a masterful design. The anatomy of the night played well into dawn. Our bodies can now rest asleep, while the heat moved on.

JAZZED

A Love Supreme is one of My Favorite Things.
I Countdown my Village Blues.
As the sun embrace me in A Sentimental Mode.
My soul is caressed in Central Park West.
What a test to be blessed with words of manifest.
A song in melody
Whispers a tune in Blues Minor.
The love of my life is my mission to find her.
And deliciously remind her.
Without regret, I take Giant Steps,
To emotionally intertwine with her.
The design of my wisdom is blazed
Over Crescent moon skies.
Filled with Bessie Blues eyes.
Evergreen trees,
Greensleeves,
And Naima's scented breeze.

I'm cooling' out like that.
I'm chilling' out like that.
Mile's Mode got my vibes like that.
Nancy (With the Laughing Face)
Invited me into her intimate space.
And played me like Tenor Sax,
As I craved for a second taste.
I palmed and held her rhythm
In my chocolate hands.
While JC played What's New
Throughout the night.
Listening to Say It, Cousin Mary, and Mr. Knight.
We alternated beats and exchanged sweets.
Echoing in the dark.
Dancing in the park.
The love of my life is fondling my frame.
Mr. Africa is my brother's name.

I lay in the wish of my tender bliss.
And pay homage to his style and game.
I am Jazzed off the sounds of John Coltrane.

MARRIAGE CARAMEL HILLS

Querida Karen,

Marriage is essential and sentimental. I do not blindly approach this. Here are my credentials. Tall, dark, and fine. You were born to be mine. Leader, wise, and strong. I will never guide you wrong. I am built to give it to you butt naked and deep into you raw. You are the finest woman that I saw. You are beautiful and complete. You are my woman and I am your super freak. I am pulled towards you in the light or in the dark. Our flame started from a spark. I can see you with my touch. I can feel you with my eyes. I can hear you with my tongue. Spread your legs wide open and I can eat you until you cum. Not once. Not twice. Three times at least. If you nut in my mouth more than that. Then that's a real Muthafuckin feast. You taste sweet as Caramel that is attached to my lips. My mouth is wide open while I am holding your hips. Your love flows and circulate through my body. You are a part of me. Can't you see that you are my fantasy? My fantasy is my reality. In this life I need you next to me. Whatever your choice. Be it the red pill or the blue pill. You are the woman that makes what I am feeling, real. You are the woman that I want to share a house in the Hills.

Ya Tu Sabes,
Arturo Poetico

JUST HOLD ME TIGHT

Dear Yoni,

Place your hand on my heartbeat and grab a hold of my soul. Do not let me go for I would not be in control. You have my emotions in the palm of your hand. Be gentle with me and hurt me not. I am fragile although I am strong as steel. Just hold me tight and keep us real. You keep me in passion and loving your footsteps. Rose petals I will spread across the path that you walk. My fingers will trace the landscape of your body. Just hold me tight and allow us to be naughty. I am attracted to every inch of your flesh. I am addicted to the taste of your breast. Can you feel the heat of my breath? Can you feel the wet of my mouth? You are soft and supple in every inch of my touch. Just hold me tight. I love you so much. I am holding you tight in the shower. I am holding you tight as we make love in the rain. I am holding you tight with all my power. Just hold me tight and you will never feel pain. I am holding you tight because you are my lifeline. I am holding you tight because your kisses are sublime. I am holding you tight because in your arms I am complete. Just hold me tight and stay between our sheets. You are my blessing. You are my wisdom. I gravitate to and around you like a moon in orbit. If ever you should lose your smile. I promise that I will restore it. If ever you are sad. I promise to absorb it. I adore you with every second in time. I am yours and you are mine. You are the reason that I wake to restart each passing day. From the moment I saw you I knew I would feel this way. I am in love with you in the morning, noon, and night. In this life all I need is for you to just hold me tight.

The Best is Yet to Cum,
Poetic Art

Little Black Book

HER

Dear Jai,

My heart is bright, and my mind is clear. I think about how I am inspired by love and not fear. I must verbalize to you about how I am mesmerized by you. I feel you in my embrace although I cannot see your face. I see with the love in my heart. I hear you whispering in my mind. I can taste the purity in your friendship. To feel you is to feel the touch of the sun sprinkled over heaven. To smell you is like inhaling a field of verbena. Aromatic and refreshing like a cup of chamomile tea that is pleasing to my soul. I would hug your shadow if I could. If I could hold your reflection in my arms I would. You are my secret paradise. You are my lonely vice. If you want to sail away forever, I would not have to think twice. I am here and you are there. It makes no never mind about the past. What matters is the future that we share.

Keep it Real,
Poetic Art

I AM

Dear Tameka,

I am smooth. I am cool. I am calm. I minimize anxiety. I put stress inside my palm. In my stride I glide as I walk. The best use of my tongue is not when I talk. Sound vibrates all around when I am kissing your pussy lips. I stimulate and manipulate blood flow to your clit. My wordplay is my foreplay. In my mind I find you and I in Kama Sutra. In the flesh I know you best. I know what positions suits ya. I generate your wet flow. I penetrate and enter you deep. Sho nuff, I got the glow. It is my pleasure to get your knees weak. I can feel your pulse rising from the words I speak. This is a 12-round lesson. This is your first-round session. I am calm. I am smooth. I am cool. If I allow you to leave my life. I am a maximized fool.

One Love,
Poetic Art

BLISS AIR CHOCOLATE

Strip away my senses,

And I would still find my life with you.

If my eyes be without vision,

I would continue to navigate and journey through.

You are thoroughly detailed in the depths of my mind.

Even in triple darkness I can see you clear and fine.

This Bliss is legitimately increasing the beat of my heart.

My myocardial oxygen demand is elevating off the chart.

Rapid is my breathing because you take my Air away.

In all four seasons my love for you

Is the reason that I feel this way.

But I remain alive because I have inhaled your essence.

Your sweet aroma and your effervescence.

You are circulating within me, giving me a new life.

You are the best friend that I have always needed.

My lover and my wife.

The sun is warming, but I prefer your touch.

You tantalize my flesh and heat me up.

You have completed me and made me whole.

I am full of joy when making love to your soul.

Loving your thoughts. Your anatomy and physiology.

By order of divine, you are a part of me.

I am your Chocolate man.

I will forever palm your body in my ebony hands.

Delicate and tender. September, I remember.

We have come a long way from one, nine, eight, and two.

The best part of our start is the both of us now saying, "I do".

BLACK FIST

I spit fire from my belly and activate my black fist.
I breathe life into my rhyme and my stance is an activist.
What is this?
Who is that?
In the cover of darkness,
I only see black.
There is a trickle, when you tickle
My chocolate pickle.
You take my mind off my mind
And leave my soul sublime.
I will not be distracted,
By your sexual tactics.
But I cannot deny that I am attracted
By the trap that you have crafted.
To lay me, you don't have to play me.
In my life, my vice has no price.
In my death, my struggle,
Will be resurrected twice.
I sip herbal teas,
Living in modern day prophecies.
With a lemon twist.
Without shackles caressing my wrist.
I am today what I was born to be.
I am in a cage, although I am free.
I spit fire from my belly and activate my black fist.
I breathe life into my rhyme and my stance is an activist.

I FOUND MYSELF, NOT U

Dearest Art,

I have been used and abused for so long that I have lost the value of myself. I have been mistreated and made to feel weak. But I am quite strong. My heart's desire has lied and conspired to hurt me. By settling for less than my worth has stunted my growth. I realize that I am recycling dysfunction for us both. It is unfair that I have been in despair with this facade that I wear. Ignoring what is obvious. While giving attention to what is obnoxious. In my lonely time of my solitude is where I have rediscovered and fell in love with who I am once again. I love myself and can no longer settle for less. I am now awakened from a nightmare. I am now walking in clarity with perfect resolution. To my pain and suffering I've always had the solution. I am royalty. I am a beauty. I am a classy woman who has more to offer than an attractive booty. I am a priceless jewel. I am the best of God's creation. I am the mother of civilization and my body is not for your recreation. I thought I found life with you. However, I was mistaken. I am pleased and thankful that I recognize the truth. I am pleased and humbled by the person that I truly am. Many of days I have spent with my eyes in tears and feeling blue. The best thing that I can say today is that I found myself, not u.

Thank You,
Giselle

THE TONE OF YOUR FLESH

The tone of your flesh

Feels best when it is pressed against mine.

Sensual expressions of our love stopping time.

The tone of your flesh

Feels best when our bodies are intertwined.

Igniting and sparking electrical fireworks in my mind.

The tone of your flesh

Feels delicate and gentle.

Pulling out of me emotions that are sentimental.

The tone of your flesh

Is the perfect complement to that of my own.

Feeling the passionate bliss of how our life together has grown.

The tone of your flesh

Fits securely in the palm of my hand.

Feeling the strength of my fingers

Tracing your body's southern land.

The tone of your flesh

Fill me with life in my lungs.

The tone of your flesh

Is sweet like cane sugar dancing on the tip of my tongue.

The tone of your flesh

Feels soft like your kiss on my lips.

The tone of your flesh

Feels good when holding your hips.

I love everything about the tone of who you are.

I love you completely

With or without emotional or physical scars.

More than just the flesh that carries the best of you.

I love the time alone when it's just us two.

The tone of your flesh is the keeper of your mind and heart.

I miss you dearly when we are apart.

LET THE TRUTH UNFOLD (TRUTH SMOKE SWEET PEACE)

Let the Truth unfold.
Let our story be told.
The Smoke is now clear and it's time to cheer.
I have stretched my arms and hands through time.
To reach back and claim what has always been mine.
That be you my dearest.
I must be brave and fearless.
And tell you what my feelings are nearest.
I have the greatest joy when I soak into your tenderness
And bathe me in your loveliness.
Although I am alive.
My life did not begin until our connection was revived.
With you my soul and heart has been revitalized.
When I gaze upon you my eyes are perpetually mesmerized.
When I embrace you. My body is tantalized.
Let the Truth be so Sweet.
You have added a melody to my heartbeat.
Let your Sweet be my Peace.
You shine bright on me like the sun rising from the east.
The love is real and this I know you can feel.
I am your man and I am like no other.
I know you love this chocolate motherfucker.

THE WATER IS FINE (I THINK I'LL SOAK INTO YOU)

Dear Renee,

What kind of guarantee can I give you? What type of peace can I give your mind? What is the frequency of your rhythm? What is in your special place that I should find? I have been merely getting my feet wet in the spiritual, mental, and emotional body of your deep waters. It is however now that I am standing here naked and unashamed ready to dive into the center of your depth. For so long I have had imageries of you, and I entangled with the joys of one another. I see you very clear. I hear you very real. I taste you very wet. I touch you very warm. I smell you very thoroughly inhaling all your form.

Joyful Love,
Poetic Art

PICTURE CORAL FOOLED SMILE

I can see and Picture us together forever.

Passion under the stars. Loving in midnight bliss.

Living for the suppleness of your tender kiss.

I can see us forever together.

Sunset evenings reflecting a pinkish orange hue.

Illuminating the color spectrum across a sky of blue.

With your eyes sparkling gentle and warming me to my core.

The love I have for you I have never experienced before.

I can see you and I together. Me and you forever

Skinny dipping off the beach shore waters.

Holding with you hand by hand.

Walking with you side by side.

A wonderful life besets us together.

Involving and evolving the union of our lives.

I can see me and you

Standing in colors Coral.

Saying I do.

Saying I will.

Saying yes forever.

Saying we are one together.

I can see the best of us.

Never allowing us to be Fooled or led astray.

Never allowing our love to be fractured or broken.

Be it night or day.

Be it dry or wet.

Be it hot or cold.

With you I will grow old.

I can Picture and see us together forever.

Simple words can never fully express what you mean to me.

You excite and fulfill every fiber of my body.

You ignite and define the depths of who I am as a man.

With a Smile on my face

I am yours yesterday, tomorrow, and in the present time.

Lock me away if love be my crime.

From the moment I first saw you I knew that you would be mine.

NEW COMFORT SECURITY CONSCIOUS

I woke up just in time to see the sun rising over
    Wilmington and El Segundo.
The air is crisp with a twist of lavender in its scented breeze.
It is a New day and I am ready to go.
I check the hour on my wrist, and I am at ease.
I am refreshed and cannot wait to see her.
She has always shined brighter than anyone else.
Warming the depths of my heart and electrifying my mind.
My spirits are high, and I melt from her seductive shine.
I see in her a beauty that others do not see nor do they appreciate.
My destiny awaits me, and I cannot be late.
She releases a Comfort within me that is unexplainable.
I never imagined that a life with her would be attainable.
Time has been kind to me and allowed she and I a purity.
The past is behind me and she and I have Security.
I am hers and she is mine.
I am handsome and she is fine.
We are one with a soul sublime.
Our life is real, but it feels more like a dream.
Our touch is tangible and it's everything that it seems.
I am awake and Conscious of what I am blessed with.
I do not take her as common
Because she is not to be messed with.
It is what it is so you might as well put this on your list.
This world is ours. I love you Ms. Criss.

MI NOMBRE

Querida Mariposa,

Mi nombre es Arturo. Pero no siempre fue así desde el principio. A través de tiempos felices y corazones rotos. Las cuerdas de nuestro corazón se han desgarrado. He estado corriendo por el tiempo en mi mente como un maratón. Aferrarse a los recuerdos de ti que están cerca y claros. Pensamientos sobre ti nunca se irán. Si alguna vez estás perdido. Te encontraré navegando por los mapas estelares. Iluminando la oscuridad como una diosa del sol. En sus marcas. Prepárate y vete. Vamos a reiniciar esto. Te extraño y te anhelo de nuevo. Aprender de nuevo será mi misterio. Amarte de nuevo es mi destino. Mi nombre es Arturo y te necesito a mi lado.

Ya Tu Sabes,
Arturo Poetico

TAMMY

Tammy, Tammy, Tammy.

Within my mind, body, and soul

Is the best of me. To you I give of me.

I have been looking for you my entire existence.

Without knowing what or who you would be.

The passion burns persistent and consistent

For your attributes and qualities.

I am pleased with who I see. Moreover, my breath has been
taken away.
I am stunned and amazed by the design that God has chosen for
you.
I see beneath the surface of your flesh and into the purity of your
spirit.
If I place my hand over your heart, I can not only feel it, I can
hear it.
In looking at you my sight has been blessed with a vision that is
true.

Life can be fleeting and at times like a vapor.

Dissipating before clarity has set in.

Before one can seize the moment of truth.

Before tender touching and embracing

The object of my affection.

For this, it is upon my heart's desire

To leap into your direction.

I feel like time has been reversed.

Without words to rehearse.

Do you like me? Mark 1 for yes and 2 for no. I like you Tammy.
So, I mark 1.
You are refreshing. The embodiment of true blessings. So, I
mark 1.
You are peace of mind and I can feel your comfort caressing. So,
I mark 1.
Your smile is infectious, and your voice is soothing. So, I mark
1.
Love is beholding to the journey of life that will not be treated as
common.

Tammy is no common woman.

And I am no common man.

Tammy, Tammy, Tammy.

I am pleased and honored to know thee.

I completely feel your warmth the way I feel the sun.

Our friendship is essential for the best of we.

Within my soul, body, and mind.

I love you completely and you have the best of me.

So, I mark 1.

CAN I SPEND MY LIFE WITH YOU?

Can I share my life with you?

Can we build something new for just us two?

How sweet life is with you next to me.

Precious joys navigate the expressways of my heart.

If I describe to you how each day gets sweeter with you.

I would never know how to start.

You are my blessing that has manifested over time.

The sun has baked you inside the sweetest thoughts of my mind.

I am grateful. I am thankful.

My heart is full, and my eyes swell with happiness.

I miss you when we are apart.

It is an agony that builds to an ecstasy

When you come back to me.

You are uncut. You are pure.

The sweetest love that I endure.

I love you deeply.

I say this with pride.

We could live three lifetimes

And I would still have so much love inside.

I do not take you for granted.

Not a second. Not a minute.

Without you I do not know how I would stand it.

You are the woman of my dreams

Whether I be awake or sleep in bed.

Will you marry me Tammy Criss?

And that's all that needs to be said!

SWEET DRIP

Fingertips and Sweet lips.

Swaying hips and Back dips.

Massaging on your supple clit.

In your inner thighs is where my tongue flips.

Inside your pussy is where my dick fit.

I am rocking your body with a firm grip.

My words are on point and I am not off scrip.

However, I will go off script and take you on a magic trip.

Do not worry about a fall or slip.

You remain on my radar blip.

If you cannot take the full shaft, I will just give you the tip.

If you take it full blast, you will have a sweet wet drip.

BEFORE THE ORGASM (ACROSS THE ROOM)

I see her from across the room.
I'm looking at her and she's smiling my way.
She's throwing me signals and I'm feeling the vibe.
She looks like the kind of woman that can birth my tribe
Beautiful in every way that I can see.
My mind briefly ponder what fate has in store for me.
I shake my thoughts and walk the path that is in her direction.
I make my approach and clear my throat.
As I make contact and ask her name.
She speaks softly and peaceful. Serene and calm.
She replied to me that her name is Lavon.
I felt a layer of warmth upon me.
As if I was feeling the rays of the sun for the first time.
We connect like beads on strings.
We talk of royalty and passion.
We talk about our first kiss and Queens and Kings.
I am captivated and gravitate on her every word.
My mind is bursting with mental ejaculation.
My soul is on fire from her verbal masturbation.
Enchantingly fine from her appearance to her spirit.
Erotic tensions scream loud in our eyes.
And our bodies can hear it.
We listen to our bodies and do what we must.
She leads me to the way of love and maybe lust.
If a be the way that I am, and the way that I be.
This kiss of bliss will keep us happy.

CAN WE TALK?

Hey baby, can we talk?
I've been noticing how fine you are.
Your eyes, thighs, hips, lips, and the way you walk.
Damn! You got me in a trance.
The smell of your scent alone makes my nature dance.
We've never met, but you know me well.
I have many names, but you can call me Heat.
You feel me in the day and in the night but never speak.
I'm the arousal between your thighs.
I'm the warmth in your eyes.
When you're hot, it's me massaging your spot.
I'm the friction inside your addiction.
Baby I need to get with you.
Can we meet? Can I taste you from head to feet?
If you were wine, I'd be drunk.
Allow me inside so I can freak your funk.
Hey baby, can we talk?
I've been noticing how fine you are.
Your smile, style, and curves.
Your sultry legs, and how that ass swerves.
I will show you tonight when your nipples peak.
    I'm the real deal. I'm Heat the freak.
    I will put you to bed and lay you to sleep.
Hey baby, please understand that my talk is not cheap.

DAMN (I SAY)

I say damn!
Don't put it on me so tight.
Let me kiss you up your thigh and love tongue you all night.
As I sip from your lips you taste good in my mouth.
I like the way you move that ass north to south.
I say damn!
You are so fine.
You are sweet like sugar and hot like wine.
Every time I see you, it's like a brand-new day.
Every time I leave you, it's painful to say.
You are my life love. From the start to finish.
My feelings for you will never diminish.
I say damn!
You put it on me just right.
I'm a slave for your love and will do whatever you like.
Let me undress your body from your silk and lace.
Damn it feels good when I enter your space.
Keep heating it up and never cool it off.
Don't stop the love even when you make my nature get soft.
As I inhale the scent of your body, you smell like a rose.
I say damn!
The way you make me curl up my toes.

BREEZE RING GOD TIME

Allow me to take my time with you.

And not just Breeze through.

The pathway to our love is not paved with haste.

In this season of our life we do not have time to waste.

Our journey obliges us to take an adequate pace.

I desire to be in moments with you admiring the smile upon your face.

Taking time out for us to be happy in our private and secluded space.

I adore you and I must openly confess.

That you give me butterflies

And throttle the beat of my heart within my chest.

Ride me slow or drive me fast.

It does not matter. Just don't crash.

Drive me hard or ride me smooth.

Either way you choose. I cannot lose.

Because I am with you and you are with me.

Bless me emotionally, lovingly, and intimately.

As I will always continue to give to you the best of me.

God has guided us to be in each other's company.

Let us not hesitate on our choices and decisions.

We have already suffered lost time like an inmate in prison.

The blessing is the lesson that we must learn.

We have neglected our own joy.

So now it's our turn.

Hold my hand and together we will grab our Ring.

It is our ultimate prize and it is the real thing.

My Ring is yours and yours is mine.

Your name has been etched up and down my spine.

Allow me to take my time and profess all my love to you.

We are now one and used to be two.

The pathway of our love is that you are my best friend.

Our journey in this season of our life, obliges us that we have no End.

CAUGHT MY EYE (GOLD SAND PICTURE CONCRETE)

I walked by your table and you caught my eye.

Simply in your space with no one's attention at play.

I looked at you and was taken by surprise.

I was stuck standing still and mesmerized by you.

I felt like a man looking into the sun at its brightest time of day.

You are amazingly beautiful, and I was momentarily blinded.

I felt heated and warm from your physical display.

My respirations diminished as you took my breath away.

My mind quickly created a kaleidoscope

Of words to interpret my emotions

You looked to be the embodiment of all my devotions.

I felt like I had discovered Gold.

And not just any.

The type of rare Gold that has been sought out by many.

Overlooked and not recognized.

I have an eye for recognition.

When I saw your face, I knew my heart would be in submission.

I desired to hold your body in my hands

The way that an hourglass holds Sand.

While keeping the seconds and minutes of time well protected.

I wondered if I was the type of man

That would be selected to walk with you.

To build with you. To heal with you. To live, cry, and die for you.

My mind continued to create a tapestry

Of endless possibilities of love and life.

A portrait Picture of man and wife.

I stood firm standing on my foundation.

Feeling an enormous amount of joyful sensation.

The moment had come for me to introduce myself and speak.

Although I was nervous, and you had my knees weak.

I knew I needed to be as strong as Concrete.

What do I say?

How do I try this?

I simply said hello.

My name is Elias.

DARK TRUST WATER LUST

Every day I win.

I am blessed that I was birthed in my Dark skin.

The day that I leave this life.

Resurrect me in Dark skin all over again.

The royalty of my flesh connects me to the Most High.

In God I Trust.

Face to face and eye to eye.

I am dipped and dripped in Dark chocolate richness.

If you are not born of the sun

Then you cannot handle my thickness.

I am like stainless steel, so I do not rust.

If we be one, then Trust is a must.

Do not hesitate if you know what you want,

And you want what you know.

If you study long, you will study wrong.

I am steady hard, and steady strong.

My love for you is wider than all oceans combined.

The depth of my love for you, no one can find.

You are deeply ingrained within the recesses of my mind.

Your Flesh on my flesh. Our bodies stay intertwined.

Not just the physical. But in every way that is known.

You are my Queen and I am your King seated on our throne.

With every breath we take. We keep happiness in our home.

Every night I win.

I am blessed that I have you in my life to embrace my Dark skin.

You are the natural necessity that I need.

In the same way that I need Water.

You are essential to me.

Spiritually, emotionally, and mentally.

How many times must I speak to you with words so sweet?
Always.

How many times have you filled my heart with heat?
Forever.

I think I should tell you this and remove interpretations.

You are my woman and I love you in my sleep.

But there is more to this thing we have, and the Water runs deep.

You are my woman and I also Lust for you from head to feet.

NUESTROS CUERPOS

Querida Luciana,

Soy débil mientras hablo sobre los movimientos sexuales de tu calor latino. ¿Soy un bebé llorón? Tal vez. Mientras lloro a tus pies El amor que hacemos está por encima de todo lo que puedo soportar. Susurras palabras en mi oído que los dulces cubren las paredes de mi mente. Mi cerebro renace. Las dendritas y las sinapsis se están sobrecargando. Mi cuerpo se está vaciando dentro de ti repetidas veces. Estoy explotando y recargando. Cortocircuitas mi sistema nervioso central en cada golpe de calor. Me obligas a alimentarme el coño y me pides que no me ahogue. ¿Cómo es eso posible cuando mi cara está empapada? Eres mi reina Azteca que se ha manifestado desde mis sueños. Caminando y hablando a todo color. Soy tu rey Zulú gimiendo los sonidos de placer de tus labios a los míos. Así es como estábamos destinados a ser. Desde el momento en que te hablé palabras de interés. Sé que estaríamos bien.

Ya Tu Sabes,
Arturo Poetico

IN MY JUNGLE

A bowl of vegetables and fruits.
A dance of Ashanti
In my jet-black boots.
The sun shines bright
On my nappy roots.

Peace. Yah bless, caress me.
I love my people endlessly.
An ancient chant. An ebony song.
I feel the groove and the beat.
From my ancestors' drums.

In my Jungle I be free.
In my village is where I be.

Mother, wife, son, daughter.
The essence of life
Flows through water.

Father, husband, sister, brother.
We drink from
The life of each other.

I roll up my sleeves
And pull up my straps.
I carry my family on my back.

If I be weak, they be strong.
If I be strong, we move on.

PEACH

Dear Rebecca,

My peach feels firm in my hand. It is neither over ripened nor removed too soon. It is just right for consumption. As I raise my peach towards my lips. Its tasty aroma is gently wafting inside my nostrils. Before ever the peach embrace my lips, it has consumed my body from the inside out. What a delight to my system. As I bite into this perfect peach, I feel a wetness about my mouth. It is the perfect temperature. Not overly gushing with its juices. Not withholding its adequate natural wet taste and flavors. As consumption continues. The texture of its flesh feels like a lingering passionate kiss. My peach feels grainy on my tongue. Grainy as if sugar was placed there now dissolving in my mouth. Its flesh is deliciously addictive all the way to its core. All my taste receptors are welcoming this experience. Sweet is my satisfaction. Fulfilled is my reaction. My peach has left residue on my lips with savory sweet flavors for remembrance.

Sweet Love,
P A

THAT'S MY PEACH

That's my Peach.
That's my Pussy.
I open you up and you are very Juicy.
Let your nectar drip drop all over me.
I am your trick.
You are my treat.
From your candy sweets that you secrete.
It is my pleasure to freely dive into you.
You will never have to push me.
When I plunge
I get sprung
From your pearl tongue.
You remain wet and gushy.
I could eat you for hours.
Yes.
That pussy I will devour.
Yes.
I could eat you for days.
Yes.
That peach got me in a daze.
Yes.
I capture you on my bottom lip.
I sip the residue of your taste.
It reminds me of corn syrup.
High fructose cum on my tongue.
I am kissing you below your waist.
T to the A to the M M Y.
I tell you to get on all fours.
And you know God damn why!
I approach my Peach from the back.
And put my heat on your clit.
As long as I have a face.
You will always have a place to sit.
That's my Peach.

THE BERMUDA PUNANY

I cannot fight nor flee from your arrangements and angles.

I cannot escape the grasp and depth of your three-sided box.

The way you grip and twist me.

You got me on lock.

Without the key I am being sucked in, and I am now entangled.

My Isosceles pleasure.

My Equilateral treasure.

I am caught within your Bermuda Punany.

Intertwined in your wet currents.

Your fluids are slippery and splashing against my body.

Trickling and dripping about my rod and staff.

Flowing up and down the sides of my chocolate shaft.

I have made it inside the mystery and legend of your longitude.

I have tapped into the center of your latitude.

Side. Angle. Side.

I get lost between your thighs.

I get lost looking into your eyes.

I can never be found while my face is down.

That is a fact and true. Down on you.

Sucking your Punany and licking your Juice.

This is a victory. There is no truce.

Drinking your Nectar and sucking your clit.

There is no loser. This is legit.

Your Bermuda taste delicious and your Triangle is my treat.

Your Punany stays wet and you secrete so sweet.

If I be lost in, you forever.

Let this be my fate to meet.

SPARE ME

Spare me your words.
I don't want to hear your shit.
Spare me your lies.
Our flame is no longer lit.
You took me for granted.
I could no longer stand it.
We have been headed on a path to collision.
Spare me your tears.
This is the right decision.
This journey has exhausted its shelf life.
You played me wrongfully.
You are less than a wife.
Spare me your concern.
You have treated me as common.
History is for us to learn.
Our fire no longer burns.
The passion no longer yearns.
You have played out of turn.
Spare me your time.
I have wasted mine.
The only thing that I want from you,
Is the peace of mind
Knowing that we are through.
Spare me.

ALTERED BEAST

I am an altered beast.
To say the least.
I am ravenous and carnivorous.
My body is thick, eager, and heated.
I will take my time with you.
Such that my energy is not depleted.
You are a complete grown woman.
Well done and succulent.
My hands are sun baked with anticipation.
My fingertips are thumping
With blood for stimulation.
I am an altered beast.
I need to feed.
I tower and devour with a ferocious power.
I am patient as well as I am agitated.
Your body is teasing and tempting.
I am starving and aggravated.
I am an altered beast.
It is time to feast.
I crave sweet meat.
I own the pussy that I eat.
I am part this and I am part that.
I am the freak that comes out at night.
I am the one that climax you right.
I am an altered beast.
I do not catch and release.
I need you for my survival,
Entering inside and out of you.
I thrive to survive.
I am alive on arrival.
I am an altered beast.
I erupt long and deep.
My nature dictates
That I eat you to sleep.

QUEEN RING HOUSE

This life is the only one I have.

There is no doubt that you were born to be my better half.

I love your smile. Your style. Your laugh.

When you are next to me.

My mind plays a melody.

I love your touch. Your taste. Your lovely face.

Our House is not a home

Without us in the same space.

Harmony is always a part of me when you are near.

You are my common denominator.

You complete me and that is clear.

I am completely at your mercy to do as you please.

I am your numerator that is down on his knees.

For you I give my life. My love. My all.

You make me feel like a man ten feet tall.

For you I give my life. My loyalty. My sacrifice.

I offer you this Ring and I am asking you to be my wife.

One love. One heartbeat. One imagination.

You are my Queen. You are the real thing.

You are the manifestation of beauty from Gods creation.

Let me make this simple.

You are the best. You are my love validation.

These are my words that manifest from within my heart.

Inside my chest you ignite me from your spark.

My body is on fire. I am hot and heated.

My love for you is sharp as a razor and it is never depleted.

I will walk through hell fire for you. You are my heaven.

I thrive to stay alive. I will not be defeated.

I can verbalize all day. I can summarize all night.

The real satisfaction is in my actions.

I love you whole. I love you divided.

Fuck it! I love you in fractions.

We connect deeply all the way down to our chemical reactions.

T to Y and S to Z

I only want to walk this planet with you next to me.

LISTEN CLOSELY

Can you hear my vibrations speak?

Your smooth muscles are relaxing.

Your frequency is unique.

Your labia are unfolding.

The minora and majora.

Like a flower beholding.

Spreading for satisfaction.

Spring is in full bloom.

I am feeling the forecast.

There will be rain soon.

SAND BLACK STAR

Dear Jasmine.

When I look into your soul, I need and want you so much. When I look into your eyes, I see the sun, moon, and Stars. Oh, how I love your touch. Midnight passion and afternoon bliss are the depths of my desire for you. Morning wishes and evening kisses are my yearning sensations for us two. Your body is seductive and heavenly produced. You have my mind and body electrified and completely seduced. Your lips are delicious and nutritious for my appetite. Your hips rock me with pleasure when you ride me tight. When I kiss over you from front to back. I feel your heat. I feel you shiver as your body contracts. Everything stands still and I fade to Black. When I look at you and me. I know that we are making history. The Sand in our hourglass has not yet been filled. You should know by now that what we have is real.

Soulful Love.
Poetic Art

ORIGINAL FANTASY (PART TWO)

You are the Original Fantasy

That has always belonged next to me.

You are the Original Fantasy

That loving on you

Was meant for me.

Three times a charm.

It is meant to be.

You are my Original Fantasy.

Immeasurable words of thanks to Tammy.
To whom kept this book
in my conscious and unconscious mind.
You have helped me in the production
of this First Edition. Assisting me in every step
of the process.

www.ingramcontent.com/pod-product-compliance
Lightning Source LLC
Chambersburg PA
CBHW030151200626
46812CB00016B/1797